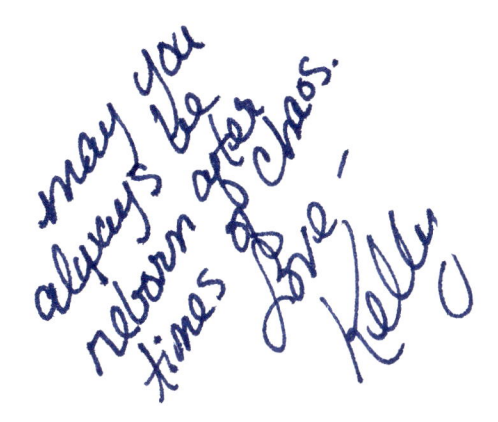

mother of chaos: queen of the nines

Poems

Kelly Clayton

Introduction by Andrew Jolivétte

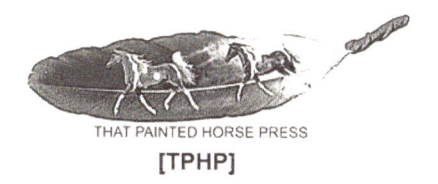

THAT PAINTED HORSE PRESS
[TPHP]

Harrah, Oklahoma
Calgary, Alberta
2020

mother of chaos: queen of the nines

© 2020 by Kelly Clayton

ISBN 978-1-928708-07-0

Except for fair use in reviews and/or scholarly considerations, no part of this book may be reproduced, performed, recorded, or otherwise transmitted without the written consent of the author and the permission of the publisher.

Introduction: Andrew Jolivétte © 2020

Cover Image: "Mama Before Coffee" © 2015 Jonathan Wilson

Author Photo Jackson Schneider©2019

Editor: Rain Prud'homme-Cranford, Executive Editor, TPHP
Editorial Assistant: Noémie Foly
Book Design: That Painted Horse Press RPC
Cover Design: Jackson D. Schneider

Native Writers' Circle of the Americas

[IPLC]
Indigenous Publishers
Literary Collective

That Painted Horse Press: A Borderless Indigenous Press of the Americas
https://thatpaintedhorsepress.blogspot.com

Acknowledgements

The following poems have appeared, in various forms and titles, in these publications. For the kindness and professionalism of each editor, I am immensely grateful.

"Cartography of a Love Affair" - *Motif Magazine*
"It's Not the Weight, But How You Carry It" - *Louisiana Creole Peoplehood: Tracing Post-Contact Afro-Indigeneity and Community*
"Our Mother, Who Art in Silence" - excerpt from original play, "Dancing with Aurora Borealis" by Kelly Clayton
"Atchafalaya Two-Step" - *China Grove Press*
"Justine Takes Off "- *FutureCycle Press*
"Magicicada" - *Gloom Cupboard, Unlikely Stories*
"Oya Dresses for Roques Dance Hall" - *The Dead Mule School of Southern Literature*
"End of the Month Red Beans & Rice" - *The Dead Mule School of Southern Literature*
"Jump In When the Rope is High" & "Grown Ass Child" - Excerpts from "Ripe Figs Don't Keep" - Choreography by Clare Cook, spoken word by Kelly Clayton

Mési, Hiweyú- with thanks:

Without a doubt, this book would not exist without Brian Schneider. During our first newlywed move, as he hefted boxes of notebooks onto the truck, he laughed, and called me a writer. I replied, "I'm not a writer. I just write." For twenty years Brian has championed, supported, pushed, pulled, cheered, and believed. For, with, and in me. Bub, you are a muse like no other.

Michael, Travis, Nicholas, and Jackson. I thank MotherFatherGod every day for these wild beings. Y'all are the threads that make up the tapestry of my life.

Diana Roubique Duvall and James Clayton, thank you for your support when I thought I couldn't do this. I appreciate the generosity it took to hold my hand through this journey. I love you, Mama and Daddy.

I light the altar in thanks to my friends. Nina, Teresa, Tracey, Arla, Stephanie, and Mia. Women need women. I ring the bell, and bow to all of you. Another bow for Dr. Mark Warner, PhD, aka The Storm. Your guidance and honesty were essential ingredients in this poetry gumbo. Cottages, house sits, airline miles, food, and huzzahs do not grow on trees. Thank you Anne and Ben Blanchet, Nina and Chris Tassin, Susan Lindsay and Michael Hesse, as well as Hilary, John, and Arla Slaughter, for your patronage.

I offer deepest gratitude to the staff and administration at VONA Voices, and Hedgebrook. VONA showed me what it feels like to belong. Hedgebrook showed me that I am a writer.

Andrew Jolivétte, Jericho Brown, Morgan Jerkins, and Thomas Parrie, I am blessed to simply write your names in this sentence. It gives me the vapors. For real.

Lastly, Rain Prud'homme. I am beyond grateful for Rain in all of her incarnations. Her ear for beauty and ferocity, combined with her exacting professionalism makes her a future Lwa of poetry. Thank you, thank you, thank you.

Dedication

For Brian, who shelters me under his arm, heartbeat crooning the song of us.
Backward and forward.
Eternal.

Content Rites

Introduction, Andrew Jolivétte..iii

Prologue

100 Lines 1

I. The Breath of Ancestors

Had Me a Good Time, Caught Me a Fine Man........................4
End of the Month Red Beans & Rice 5
Ayizan Walks Through the French Market 6
Ice Box Dancer...7
Astrodome City 8
Jump in When the Rope is High 9
Carmelite 10
Lake Arthur Stomp..11
All Music is Folk Music 12
Outhouse Meditation..13
Penniless 14
Things He Miss..15
Oya Dresses for Saturday Night at Roque's Blues Hall 16

II. This Middle World is Fire

1972 Easter Offensive...18
Because I Took A Lover 19
Super Freak 20
Corner of Poydras & Basin: Mardi Gras Morning 21
Eintou Before Swine 22
Grown Ass Child 23
Moss Piglets Will Watch the Sun Die, and Then Go Home for Supper 24
The Unfolding...26
Left Leg Strap Down..27
Justine Takes Off...28
The Party Line (on inter-family gossip)................................30

Trigger Happy World..30
Regrets, I've Had a Few..31
Working Title: Row Yo Boat...32
Oya Dances the Bamboula: Congo Square, August 2005..........33
Quitting Time at Ruth's Chris Steakhouse................................35
Magicicada...36

III. The Sweetest Place on Earth

Creole Ladies Don't Do That...38
Atchafalaya Two-Step..39
Homage to My Hips (after Lucille Clifton)...............................41
Apartments for Rent on Craigslist...42
Lagniappe..43
What Mama Do..44
The Price of Starting Over..45
Belly..46
Yesterday I Was Called A Cunt...47
Nit Picker...48
Thunder Wheels...49
Never Too Old to Fight..50
Our Mother, Who Art in Silence...51
Sugar in My Bowl: Post Menopausal Musings (after Nina Simone)..53
Cartography of a Love Affair..54

Epilogue

A Girl Turns a Doorknob...59

Introduction

In mother of chaos, queen of the nines, Kelly Clayton unearths the spirit of a dynamic and complex people. Weaving together history, storytelling, religion, gender, and culinary traditions, through free verse and poetic forms in a land based literary journey steeped in cultural traditions. Clayton moves readers to think about notions of time and space and the intricacies of Louisiana Creole peoples. Divided into three sections: "The Breath of Ancestors," "The Middle World is Fire," and "The Sweetest Place on Earth," she seamlessly transcends between spaces that create a long-storied history that has often been misunderstood: a story of post-contact Afro-Indigeneity: Louisiana Creoles. The first section of the book is marked by memory, ancestors/family, and movement. In classrooms, dances, markets, and various spaces Clayton takes readers on a journey of remembrances. Traveling across Houston, New Orleans, and Bayou landscapes she reminds us that this life in Louisiana is inextricably linked to place, music, and custom.

Mother of chaos is a conjuring. For example, in "Lake Arthur Stomp," the author conjures Amede Ardoin, one of the fathers of Creole and Cajun music. Conjuring and notions of chaos are deeply important themes well-known across the state of Louisiana, particularly in Creole communities. To conjure is to bring to light, to center, and make known that which seems unknowable. Connected to voodoo, root working, or hoodoo, conjuring comes from a long tradition of West African and Indigenous spiritual traditions creolized into forms of healing and protection (unlike popular narratives that reduce these practices to "magic"). To conjure is also to call upon a person or ancestor. Throughout the first section of this rhythmic book, Clayton conjures many ancestors and many memories to help readers remember how past is prologue. One of the most powerful aspects of the author's writing is her ability to insert political and economic issues into her analysis. For example, in "Outhouse Mediation," she reminds us of the economic differences between class groups while also signaling that joy comes in many forms, which have little to do with money and economic resources alone. On the one hand, this is a book about survivance and resilience, but I would argue that it is also a set of widely diverse tales documenting the everyday ways that Creole people in Louisiana thrive, even in the direst of circumstances. In fact, as I read through these works not only does the imagery take me to the streets of so many cities and parishes, it reminds me of the ways that our ancestors created so much from what many considered so little.

In "All Music is Folk Music (a title taken from Louis Armstrong)," Clayton yet again conjures the spirits of many intersecting dynamics from gender to class, to her major theme of chaos. She writes:

>Leaves bring the sugar down.
>Ready to drop.
>
>Gotta clean the red kettle.
>Ready to Drop.
>
>Let him play football?
>Ready to drop.
>
>He think he grown, grown, now.
>Ready to drop.
>
>Okay, where's my rent then?
>Ready to drop.
>
>And what's he bringing home for suppertime?
>Ready to drop.

Forgot to thaw the pork chops.
Ready to drop.

Guess I'm frying eggs and rice again.
Ready to drop.

Bathe the babies, clean the hamster cage.
Ready to drop.
The mirror ain't my friend today.
Ready to drop.

Lord, I need a drink.

What role has patriarchy played in a colonized state like Louisiana? What influence has a Latin-based French and Spanish culture left upon an Afro-Indigenous, mixed-blood / mixed cultural people? What is ready to drop next? What do women, Creole and other women, in Louisiana have to also be ready to pick up as a result of the structures left behind? How do they trace their next moves from our ancestors' wisdom?

If section I of *mother of chaos* is about memory and movement, then section II, "The Middle World is Fire" is about trials, tribulations, defiance, and survivance. For Creole women (and many women born and raised in Louisiana in general), these are familiar themes. Despite the overwhelming presence of Catholicism and patriarchy there is an even stronger Indigenous and Afro-Indigenous tradition that is matrilineal. It is steeped in refusal. It is embedded in doing, thriving, and being without "permission." As Clayton reveals in her poem, "Because I Took a Lover" there are no apologies, there are no particular structures of rules that can control the legacy of endurance, strength, and independence among these women in Louisiana.

Because I Took a Lover

without permission from one
in a position to grant permission...

Because I became pregnant with desire
for delusion, I lied. Daily. Wore my steam engine
apron high on my waist. Sautéed the future until time to deliver
a new reason wrapped in soft cotton...

Because the story, 37 years long, is the distance I'll walk
til I reach unpainted screen door, I won't knock.
I won't ask permission...

When she arrives at that unpainted screen door she "won't knock," because the answers are sewn into her body, into her ancestral memory. She is bearing new life and new light. She is resisting every story, trauma, and every sautéed remembrance of what patriarchy tries to conceal. Womanhood, much like concepts of peoplehood, center connections to something more than the material. Clayton amid constructions of what may be deemed chaos, demonstrates how Creole womanhood is not unlike a song, producing deep feeling: profound, painful, and joyous- all at the same time. And in the full knowing of womanhood, sorrow, and triumph we witness something else from Clayton: how self-doubt and worry leave us stranded in our own thoughts about our insufficiencies and our imperfections. As Clayton writes in "Grown Ass Child:"

> If you let loose what do you think will happen? Your fear beats the worry drum, I'll never amount to anything full or sweet
> without your help...

> Like that time you snooped, you get what you get for
> that, Hoarder of my fuckups. You ate boxes of words all in one sitting,
> which made you sick to your stomach...
>
> I won't need you to tell me how, why, when, to cross
> Easy Street. I got this.
> Wait. Hold up, don't Ma, I'm sorr... Mama? Mama?

Here Clayton asks, as we transition into adulthood how do we find and make our own paths? How do we take from what our mamas' gave us and turn that into something full? Something complete and dare I say sweet? This book reminds me of my own mother and the power to be vulnerable, but perhaps more importantly, the power to be defiant. *Mother of chaos* charts how to be independent moving societal boundaries for future generations of girls and boys who imagine themselves as chaotic, a mess, or incomplete. Clayton leads them to twirl, to tear it down, so they might dance with the mother of chaos, with Oya.

In the final section, "The Sweetest Place on Earth," the author offers another poem speaking to defiance and also to potential, in aftermath and embodiment; these central themes in the of final portion of the book. To move, defy, and embody is the take-away from this fast-paced, lyrical, and inter-generational project. Clayton is singing to a generation before and after her that to live, to experience womanhood, means to shake and rattle the cages. It also means to be unapologetic for being free and indulgent with the sweet things in life. This comes through in her poem "Creole Ladies Don't Do That."

> ...We dig past pineapple, sliced mango, red grapes,
> for a plastic bowls of cut watermelon...

> We walk the sidewalk, shade side, and eat it with our hand...
> We talk and eat, and walk, mouths open.
> We eat and grin big.
> In public.
> Just like common debris.

Throwing off every chain and every socially, politically, and culturally constructed notion of womanhood, *mother of chaos* dares us to transcend, push back, and to celebrate. Clayton dares us to own our past, present, and future while living in joy and shouting when the storms come and tides rise. In every cautionary moment of fear, she invites us to let the chaos in and make us better people for having weathered the storm.

~Andrew Jolivette
(Creole/Atakapa-Ishak [Tsikip/Opelousa Clan]),
San Diego, California, 2020

Prologue

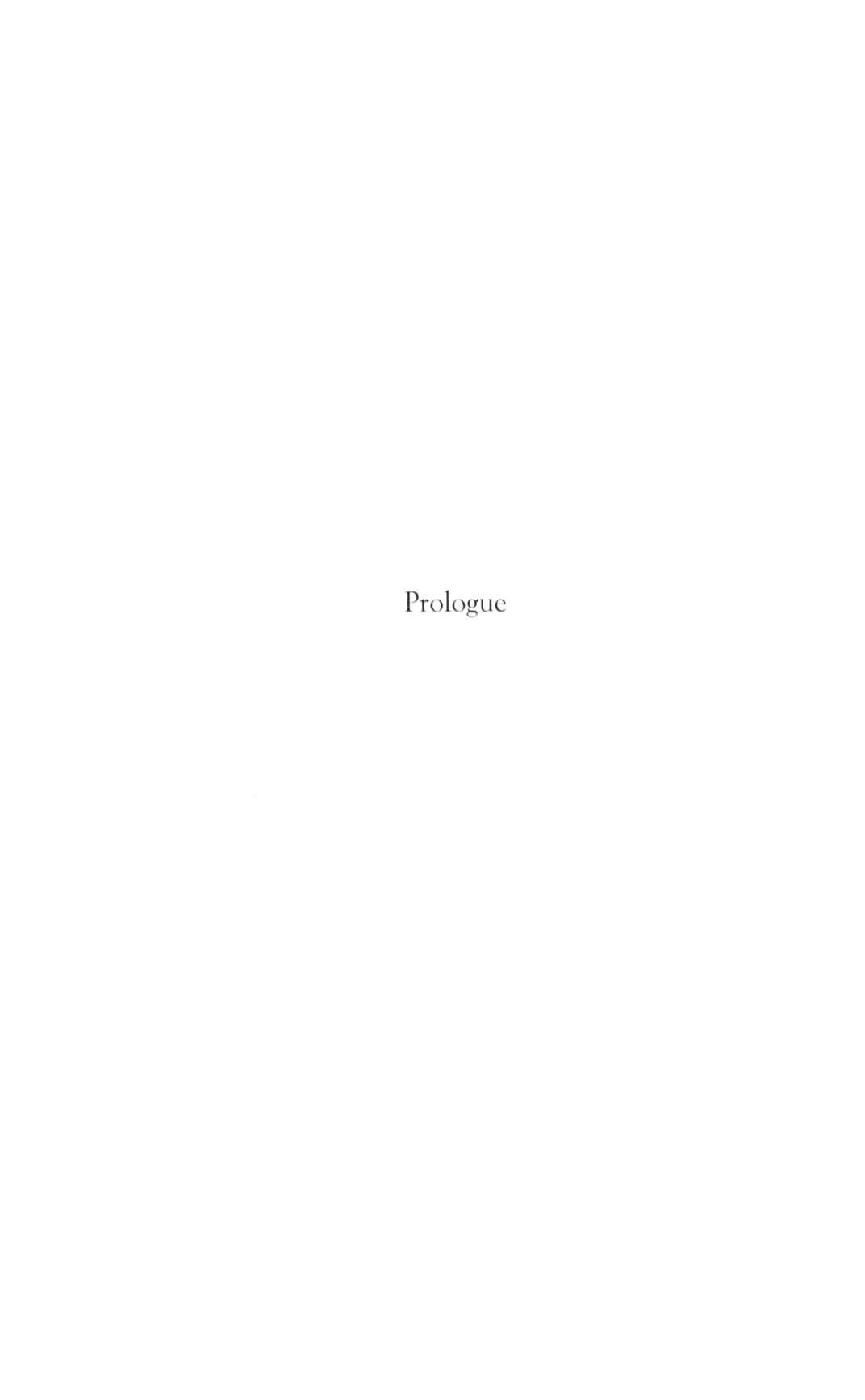

100 Lines

I must not twirl in class. I must not twirl in class. I must not twirl in class. I must not   twirl in class. I must not twirl in class. **Sorry to bother you.** I must not twirl in class. I must not twirl in class. I must not twirl in class. I must not twirl in class. I must not twirl in class. **Fainted, um, sort of. but she wasn't hurt.** I must not twirl in class. I must not twirl in class. I must not twirl in class. I must not twirl in class. I must not twirl in class. I must not twirl in class. I must not twirl in class. **Called her to my desk.** I must not twirl in class. I must not twirl in class. **Late homework.** I must not twirl in class. I must not twirl in class. **Didn't want to embarrass her.** I must not twirl in class. I must not twirl in class. I must not twirl in class. I must not twirl in class. **She spun.** I must not twirl in class. **Faced the class.** I must not twirl in class. I must not twirl in class. I must not   twirl in class. I must not twirl in class. **Held onto my desk.** I must not twirl in class. I must not twirl in class. I must not twirl in class. I must not twirl in class. **And lowered herself to the floor.** I must not twirl in class. I must not twirl in class. I must not twirl in class. I must not twirl in class. I must not twirl in class. I must not twirl in class. I must not twirl in class. **Classmates rushed to her.** I must not twirl   in class. I must not twirl in class. I must not twirl in class. I must not twirl in class. I   must not twirl in class. **Kneeled by her side, noticed she had one eye open.** I must not twirl in class. I must not twirl in class. I must not twirl in class. **Yes. Distracting.** I must not twirl in class. I must not twirl in class. I must not   twirl in class. I must not twirl in class. **She can't sit still.** I must not twirl in class. I must not twirl in class. I must not twirl in class. I must not twirl in class. I must not twirl in class. **Believes skirt pleats are there for one reason.** I must not twirl in class. I must not twirl in class. I must not twirl in class. I must not twirl in class. I must not twirl in class. I must not twirl in class. **You'll make sure she has it tomorrow?** I must not twirl in class. I must not twirl in class. I must not twirl in class. I must not twirl in class. I   must not twirl in class. **How about day after? It's a lot of work.** I must not twirl in class. I must not twirl in class. I must not twirl in class. I must not twirl in class. I must not twirl in class. **Oh? Even if she has to stay up all night?** I must not twirl in class. I must not twirl in class. I must not twirl in class. I must not twirl in class. I must not twirl in class. **Well, You're her mother.** I must not twirl in class. I must not twirl in class. I must not twirl in class. I must not twirl in class. I must not twirl in class. I must not twirl in class. I must not twirl in class. **No. Thank you.** I must not twirl in class. I must not twirl in class. I must not twirl in class. I must not twirl in class. **Goodbye.** I must not twirl in class. I must not twirl in class. I must not twirl in class. I must not twirl in class. I must not twirl in class. I must not twirl in class. I must not twirl in class.

I. The Breath of Ancestors

Had Me a Good Time, Caught Me a Fine Man

Had me a good time, caught me a fine man
but you know they say all good things
must be gon' rain cause I taste iron
Legba nan baye-a! Almost ready to come home.

But you know, they say all good things
end up on the floor, felled by the sweep of skirts
Legba nan baye-a! Almost ready to come home.
He say, "I'm married now. Do not send for me."

End up on the floor felled by the sweep of skirts
no more cane syrup tongue, he snaps, wet cloth on bare thigh
he say, "I'm married now. Do not send for me."
Two daughters, poteaux cut for grand maison, stumble run like bear cubs.

No more cane syrup tongue, he snaps, wet cloth on bare thigh
I ain't one to mess with. He gon' do right whether he want to, or not.
Two daughters, poteaux cut for grand maison, stumble run like bear cubs.
Legba nan baye-a! Almost ready to come home.

I ain't one to mess with. He gon' do right whether he want to, or not.
Must be gon' rain, cause I taste iron.
Legba nan baye-a, I'm ready. Take me home.
Had me a good time, caught me a fine man

End of the Month Red Beans & Rice

Between shifts, I sit in church. It's peaceful, quiet, free
air conditioning. Kneelers good foot rests, every bowed head
in this joint wear a net.

Mary got a job, too. Standing
glossy-still, while old ladies shove folded dollars
in the tin box by her knees. They push buttons,
light electric candles, and pray.

Get the law off Linda's man, watch over Uncle Boo's
MRI, make Ernestine's wild daughter stay home. Need money,
so tired of end-of-the-month-red-beans&rice.
Bet Mary feels for customer service.

Wonder if she walks Jesus by Temple Shalom on Wednesdays and
every other weekend. Hope she don't pack clean robes.
God can damned well buy extras to keep at His own house.
Think He drives Jesus home hours too early, or late, pulls up on
the curb at Sacred Heart, honks his trumpet for Mary to come
outside like common debris?

Or does it work beautifully for them
like it never does for the rest of us?

Ayizan Walks Through the French Market

- Hey, Mambo! Mama? I'm three, see?
- Trifling thing, not worth a fig. What do he want from me?
- Huygi piya! Sweet cane, sugar sweet cane!
- Keep moving.

Goats, sheep, pigs, swing,
a flesh corridor with human current
pulsing through colonnades.

- Boy, back off!
- Lees tu cafe' molido? Bruja Carmelita lee tu cafe!
- Don' buy coffee from nobody but Rose Nicaud.
- Scritch scratch on that l'herb a' la puce.

Coconut shell in the stream, she rests elbows, on two brothers
who tried to flow around her.
And she rides.

- Heat up some wasp mites in the bread oven, and pound into powder.
- Sugar Doo sous la merde. Get him home.
- Jus leave him where le bon Dieu flang him.
- Ta poshake! Tight enough to hold okwa!

She closes her eyes and she rides,
feet dangling, boy heartbeats tattoo
outside her thighs. She breathes collective morning
hope, 'fore it turns to smoke after sunset.

They stumble, and I lift
them off the ground, with they upper sky split
wide open, I lift, and I dust seats of pants. I lift the new morning.

Ice Box Dancer

NPR Saturday Zydeco Stomp, accordion signals,
and she pauses, head cocked, good ear up.
Creole French fills the kitchen, she grabs the handle.
Wood grain same color as his arms, her feet slide
purple socks remember the steps.

And himself.
Mr. King of the Dancehall chose his subject
blinded her with lopsided grins, wrapped her in a blanket
of promises warm from the dryer, and then cast sly eyes
on her daughter.

She lets go spins and grabs the handle again. Face unfocused
she opens outward, changes hands, twirls under her own arm.
Powerful magnetism keeps the refrigerator door closed.

Astrodome City

"Get on up now, we going for a ride."
She been drinking coffee since midnight.
I yawn, she say, "Yeah, you rite."

School tomorrow, but we gotta hide.
He may not show face, but then again, he might.
"Get on up, now. We going for a ride."

She know someone she can confide.
Kenworth Bullnose waits under street lights,
I yawn, she say, "Yeah, you rite."

George Jones autograph taped in the sleeper,
10 West to Houston, we running alright.
"Get on up, now. We going for a ride."

Breaker one nine, anyone headed to Astrodome City?
Ankle Biter calling for Silver Knight.
I yawn, she say, "Yeah, you rite."

He woulda used his fists, her head gone upside.
It's happened before. We run, no time for polite.
"Get on up, now, we going for a ride."
I yawn, she say, "Yeah, you rite."

Jump When the Rope is High

Chicory coffee, pudding pie
promised not to tell a lie.
Figgy jelly, figgy jam, golden
biscuit, side of ham

Where yo mama? Hey, ho!
Get the broom. Shoo that crow.

Round on bottom, soft inside
broke my promise, yeah I lied.
Said I'd stay forever young,
bad old crow, lay down your gun.

Where yo mama? Hey, ho!

Get the broom. Shoo that crow.

Carmelite

Church dress hangs on bedroom hook,
shoes two pairs, don't want to wear
them out, so I don't wear them at all.
On my wedding day, I forgot.

Quilts dishes, jars of muscadine wine, we couchon de lait
under dour oaks, dance until Blood
Moon singes night clouds. Maybe I took one
full breath before babies drop
from my body.

Mama sits me down Saturdays cast
iron kettle of soapy water on the porch.
She bathes my arms, legs, feet, and hair, bubbles cream bright.
I sit in the sun, close my eyes. She sings of burning cane fields

and ways to hide in plain sight.

Lake Arthur Stomp

You held out your hand asked me to dance.
No, not asked. You stood there. Knowing
I'd get up. Your green eyes, pecan pie skin
say I should be flattered, look at me like I could dig potatoes,
with my teeth and not get my nose dirty.

Amede Ardoin stirs us up, wet leaves circling a drain.
after summer rain. As we pass, you wink
at the ring of snickering work pants shouting
your name, raising they beers. You say, "Ignore them."
I duck under your raised arm. Good advice, who knows when I'll
be asked again.

Instead, I slip my hand from yours, two-step
by my damn self.

You stop, start to ease your way out, but brown water has no time
for jammed logs, and the going's slow.
Horizon, sideline safety. Almost there. Only sound louder
than Amede's accordian are stomps, howls, slapping of thighs.
Work pants ushering you off the floor.

All Music is Folk Music[1]

Leaves bring the sugar down.
Ready to drop.

Gotta clean red kettle.
Ready to Drop.

Let him play football?
Ready to drop.

He think he grown, grown, now.
Ready to drop.

Okay, where's my rent then?
Ready to drop.

And what's he bringing home for suppertime?
Ready to drop.

Forgot to thaw pork chops.
Ready to drop.

Guess I'm frying eggs and rice again.
Ready to drop.

Bathe the babies, clean hamster cage.
Ready to drop.

Mirror ain't my friend today.
Ready to drop.

Lord, I need a drink.

---

[1] title is a quote by Louis Armstrong

Outhouse Meditation

At dawn, he eats a bowl of hot cush-cush
with black syrup then leaves for cane fields.
Sun rises, our shotgun explodes
with kids. They tactac from every corner, ricochet out de back doh
to empty overnight belly bowls.

Eight his, from before, seven ours. "She stay with her drawers
down, poor thing." whispers the feed store.
At church they say I should be grateful.
Pretty, or rich, and a woman has choices.
T-Cou pulls me behind kitchen door, embarrassed
in front the older boys, but he's only three,
I still have milk, and it's free.

He say the outhouse need replacing. I say we haven't the money,
but that's not it. He wants a two seater.
Old iron hook, higher than baby arm-reach. Ignoring the stench,
I lock the door, sit and finish a drawing of a gros bec in flight.
I dream of hard candy, train rides to New Orleans,
and of buying a cow.

Penniless

If he liked to dance
you'd buy Tango shoes
and take lessons.

Was he a devoted church member?
You scrubbed your face of make-up
and became a prayer warrior.

The one that had a wife? No problem.
you met him in the Sno-ball
stand parking lot.

You believed beauty your only
currency. Your value kept in a red pocketbook
with thick lining.

Now, your purse is empty, you covet
the rich with their attached to the muscle
skin, and light filament hair.

Why don't you see that your power lies in losing
your wallet?

Things He Miss

No chér, that's not right. You can't turn the pillowcase open
end to the middle of bed. You'll get you big head stuck.
And smother.

Jesus, Mary and Joseph, look at these footprints, I just mopped
Give me that. You sweep like a monkey. No home training.
She fussed her way into this world.

Her mama told him that
on their wedding day.
Hope you know what you getting into.

Too many years turnt her vinegar to wine, to muscadine juice,
and finally to syrup. In the end, she was scent of honeysuckle
back floating on humidity, arms spread. He prays for the snap,

her obsidian eyes, when he'd leave pantry door wide open,
blessing of her undivided attention.
You make me insane, old man.
White van gone pull up soon,
and Imma hold my arms straight out
for my jacket.

Oya Dresses for Saturday Night at Roque's Blues Hall

She sits on the toilet lid, her GE make-up mirror
Day, office, home, evening, each setting lights her face rich amber.
Antelope goddess curls her eyelashes with the wind,

Dark hair wrapped in electric storm rollers
in her creamy slip she is brown pearl nail polish.
Little Bee-Eater, songless bird, watches from the doorway,
Shazam/Isis tshirt pulled over knees,

she stills veined wings so she don't get shooed
from the room that smells of hot
copper, and wild woman blankets.
Made up, Oya stands at her closet, one hand on half moon hip

Tornado of dresses twirls on her bed.
Capricious deity picks a dress of lightning, which incidentally
is the first one she tried on.
She turns toward quiet feathers, points ceremonial coat hanger
at the dress rainbow on the bed, and says,

"Chér Bebe, wanna do Mama a little favor?"

II. This Middle World Is Fire

1972 Easter Offensive

Don Cornelius invites me to the funk line.
Olive and cream braided rug, I have no goods
to swing, but I get on down. My Lazy-boy audience applauds, Ben
Gay wafts from his sleeves.
I'm in line rock stepping, waiting for my turn
to dance walk the middle.

Breaking news. Helicopters fly over grey scale
jungle mountains, Walter Cronkite says
something about Easter being offensive.
I'm shushed when I defend the holiday.

Arms folded, I shift from foot to foot, boring
men in suits talk. La, la, la, conflict. Blah, blah ground
forces. The president. Bringing them home. Treaty.
I'm ready to stomp out when Don comes back.
It's time to get on board. Love train's in the station.

Because I Took a Lover

without permission from one
in a position to grant permission
if I were to ask for it.

Because I became pregnant with desire
for delusion, I lied. Daily. Wore my steam engine
apron high on my waist. Sautéed the future until time to deliver
a new reason wrapped in soft cotton. Which I left on the Sun
porch
to be taken in and taught an epic tale of abandonment.

Because the story, 37 years long, is the distance I'll walk til I reach
unpainted screen door, I won't knock.
I won't ask permission to lean over gunmetal bassinet, lift
armload of milk plush velvet, and stuff it down
the hole in my chest.

Super Freak

After school short-order shack, I jump the counter.
Quarter in jukebox three plays, favorite song, from
my head down to my toenails. Left my spatula next
to six burgers on the grill, cheese melting in star formation,
buns traveling through conveyer rack toaster

Bounce back easy cause I hemmed my apron even
with short-shorts. I flip to the rhythm, defiant hair,
unnetted. End of shift whistle at nuclear power plant
joins chorus.

Bell on door handle jangles, burgers pre-made cause
I know what they want. Same orders every day. Cost of
a smile, and a side of hope from a girl. The kind you don't
take home to mother.

Corner of Poydras & Basin: Mardi Gras Morning

What kind of rider throws a whole bag of beads?
Ziplock full of ice on my eye, my back to the street sign, I dream
of spending Mardi Gras like a boss, invited to stay
the night on parade route, potluck dips, loaded tables, fresh solo
cups, napkins you don't have to pocket for later, when you pee
on the street.

Zulu right around the corner. This year I'll catch a coconut. Or
maybe I should take my black eye home. People are debris
this year. Grown ass men snatch beads from little kids,
Uptown rich folks set up living rooms under tents, place mark
whole blocks with interconnecting ladder chairs, right on the
curb.

I turn to go, spot three pigeons around a snickers bar lunch
counter. Another pigeon, this one raggedy patches of missing
feathers, crosses between floats, lands at the snickers. It pushes its
head between two diners and flaps elbow wings.
Startled, they hop sideways, interloper drags
whole candy bar behind a dumpster and eats it.
Alone.

Eintou Before Swine

Don't think
you something cause
they come for gumbo and
beads. If we in deep shit, don't yell
out your shotgun for them.
Cause they will not
SEND HELP

Grown Ass Child

If you let loose what do you think will happen? Your fear beats
the worry drum, I'll never amount to anything full
or sweet without your help.

Like that time you snooped,
you get what you get for that—
Hoarder of my fuckups.
You ate boxes of words all in one sitting,
which made you sick to your stomach.

So, now you know. I open jeans under sweater
before they choke me to death.
I have plenty practice. Been raising Cookie since we found her
in a boxbehind K-Mart. Even taught her to beg for treats. How
hard can it be?
You did it for fifteen years.

Not long till I move out, and up, to high rise apartment,
where I'll be killing it at my big money job.
I won't need you to tell me how, why, when, to cross
Easy Street. I got this.

Wait. Hold up, don't
Ma, I'm sorr... Mama?
Mama?

Moss Piglets Will Watch the Sun Die, and Then Go Home for Supper

He disappeared for long stretches. She phoned police station, hotels, bars, hospitals. But he didn't need one of those, he wasn't lying in a ditch, face down, whispering her name.
He always turned up with a fresh haircut and new clothes.

He measured things, hammered things, painted or unstuck stuff till she stopped fussing. No end to the things he fixed.
Bedtime, he announced "No more thumb sucking."
He held me with knees, too tight. Behind me, she washed dishes, back turned. He shoved my hand in his pants.

Wrist in a bear trap,
I struggled against steamy hardness.
Until I stopped.
Quiet.
Cold.
Still.

Shivering twice, he let go of me. I jerked oil slicked hand away, he wiped it on his jeans. Two coats paint thinner and Tabasco swabbed on my thumbs. When they dried he opened
white cotton gloves with his teeth. I went to bed, gloves duct taped to my wrists.

Night was deep space. Held in its galaxy blanket, the Dark whispered, "Child, your heart is a Tardigrade, Princess of Resilience, future Empress of Whatever it Takes."
A Water Bear is different from a land bear.
When my ring got stuck I got it off with soap and hot water.
Traps mean nothing to Moss Piglets.

Through the night sharp baby teeth broke threads until I'd torn great holes in the gloves.

I declared paint thinner and Tabasco my favorite meal,
sucked my thumbs, eyes watered, belly rolled with nausea.
Poison absorbed, body once again tasted like me.
Thumbs, portable comfort.

    The Dark, proud of her daughter, rocked me to sleep.

The Unfolding

I thought it happened in increments, our origami solar system,
once a mobile circling our heads, now a stack
of crazed paper lifted by wind. Your unchanged phone number,
giver of false hope, dangled possibilities,

or so I thought. I left messages on your birthday and Christmas.
Upped my gif game to high comedy, imagined
you barking with laughter, surprising yourself. My texts were rope
thrown into *Poltergeist* closet.

Six years later, I rehearsed your birthday message before calling.
Planned to tell you I heard that Chumbawumba
song you used to love. But we both know I'll never be arrested
for shoplifting hints.

So, I dialed. Ready with the yearly story of the day I released you,
from the star nursery. Lakeside Hospital, New Orleans,
your eyes curious, perfectly shaped head, you were a freshly fired
bisque doll. One not to be ruined by a gawky girl's dirty hands.

"The number you have reached is no longer in service. Please
check the number and dial again." I fell to my knees in the front
yard. Cars passed, a dog barked. Needle hit the record,
"I get knocked down. But I get up again.
You're never gonna keep me down."
Your sweet round face, rearview mirror, singing yourself hoarse.

Ours was not an unfolding. Now, I know for sure
that the sound of the Big Bang was a dial tone.

Left Leg Strap Down

"Arms out, wrists together." shackles for the shower.
I walk, a Geisha man, ankle chains clink
in time with his keys.
Our hallway music rolls ahead of us.

We call him LL on the walk. He think it means Louisiana
Lightning, fancies himself Angola's ambassador of death
row stand up. Every day he performs comedy bits memorized
from restricted tv, glances sideways to see if I laugh.

I always do.

We call him LL on the walk because we hear
big-man talk the guards/ LL so proud of his position
on the execution team; Left Leg Strap Down.
He wears one sleeve rolled, a frame for his scar/badge turns
it toward me, wants me to ask how he got it.

I never do.

He say he glad for new ac wall unit in that room where black
naugahyde Gumby, arms spread, waits for me.
"Room's gotta be cold. Too hard to catch sweaty
left legs." He straightens sloped shoulders, sniffs.
"That's how the scar came round, you know, toenails."

Thought I left marriage behind, the routine, her eyes, her needs
wore me out. 6x8 cell, insurance against tender-heart
diseases.

16 years, B Team 4am to noon, five days
a week longest relationship
I ever had.

Him too, I bet.

Justine Takes Off

Thirty minutes on stage, thirty working the barstools I
change into vintage corset and easy
to remove evening gown. Other girls put on make-up
razor bikini lines, count dollars falling
from glittery drawstring purses.

I slide onto a stool next to dry mouthed pez dispenser
and ask if he wants to talk — for a price.
No rest for these Pleezer platforms without sweaty
drinks in hand.

Shirley Temple every fifteen minutes means
I'll have to pee during my next set, harder to get off
the stage for hand-to-hand tips.
Mr. Dispenser's time is up. I roll onstage, carbonated
belly sloshing.

Desiree beat me to the good spot. She stares at Coke Bottle
Glasses sitting at three o'clock. She smells like peaches.

Annie Lennox asks important questions through busted speakers,
while above my head the Saints also lose
their shirts.
My bag lies on its side tied to upstage pole
while Lula Boy pulls drafts for the post office

I reach behind, touch railroad tracks in silver lame'
my dress opens, a split catfish nailed to a cypress
Give me bills held like cigarettes between two fingers
and know that the answer is yes;
I would lie to you.

The Party Line
(on inter-family gossip)

LUS Fiber says our internet is 80Mbps,
incredible bandwidth speed,
no latency. Fastest in Louisiana.
They never met our family.
Let one of us call another and drop a bomblet.
By the time we hang up, throw a load of whites in the wash,
phone lines start smoking. Auntie beeps in on sister call,
then answer cousin, and one dear friend.

Gotta go now, that's Mama.

WebMd search turns common boil into Bot Fly
nursery, ready to hatch bumble bee sized, spine covered larvae.
One moment, your shit lost, public shouting.
Now, you're viral.

Mustard gas, internet ruin, family gossip, first you detect a strange smell, then it fades, sinks inside, skin erupts, nose and throat close, suffocation complete.

Heard a click. That my brother? You gonna hafta let me go?

The brother I called morning after my fiancee's funeral where night before, I drank wine ate gumbo, cried, laughed, drank another wine. Coworker visited, offered little blue circle of comfort, which I washed down with more wine. Told brother-man I awoke, bottom naked, bloody.
Told him weeks later, doctor deletes spine covered larvae, and my trust in humanity once again.

Creole Mbps. Before spin cycle finished I am crowned,

Family Baby Killer.

Trigger Happy World
(NYT 1 February 2014, by Malone Farrow)

remind myself to breathe, I read it aloud:

"He talked to me while he did it,
whispering that I was a good girl, that this was our secret,
promising that we'd go to Paris and I'd be a star in his movies.
I remember staring at that toy train,
focusing on it as it traveled in its circle around the attic.
To this day, I find it difficult to look at toy trains."

stiff corded neck, I tip my face into cupped hands,
open-mouth scream silent — ugly
I close my eyes, send Malone a message:
I know why you changed your name.
Knee backs steam, winding tunnels of my ears itch try to shake it
off finish the essay tell myself to put on big girl panties

just words on a page:
I open the taps, feel the need for a shower ordinary raven beats
against my ribs, caws to the chorus sitting on power lines,
but the amen corner done gone home.
Water pours two steady streams, hits the heart
of my feet, falls from goose bumped breasts

adrift from my body I hover.
I am droplets of steam.
I surround the woman in the shower,
face upturned, running water, fists in armpits.
I hold her while she breathes —
hold her til she lets the raven go.

Regrets, I've Had a Few

that I told you I didn't love you
when I did

that I gave a landlord three months rent
in advance

that I pretended to like the restaurant
where you took me
to break up

the look in your eyes when I mimicked
your dancing

that I didn't slap his face, when my palm itched
and he talked, and talked,
and talked

that I said no to space travel, and cotton
candy, though in my defense

cotton candy is the only thing chickens
won't eat

Working Title: Row Yo Boat

Lawrence Ferlinghetti say rising tide lifts all boats
If you got a boat.

"You know that's right," say The People
without boats sitting on rooftops, waiting.

"It is what it is," say the family,
standing on boiling asphalt, Danzinger Bridge.

"Don't know what y'all gone do," say helicopter pilots,
"We don't respond to hand-lettered signs written in dead
language. Y'all on your own."

"But wait," The People say,
"We got us some boats. Look at this blow-up bed.
Here's an inner-tube slick as a dolphin. There go a wash tub
full of babies. Flat screen TV styrofoam keep groceries dry all day."

"We New Orleans bébé," say The People, "We gon' float."

Oya Dances the Bamboula: Congo Square, August 2005

She saunters, on break from steering fortunes in the marketplace.
Bare foot steps onto circular bricks, St. Ann and Rampart, where
time lines stack one atop the other. Gossamer transparencies.
Place des Negres, La Place Publique, Place du Cirque. Transient
labels for sacred space named by The People,

Congo Square.

Choctaw boys play raquettes against locals. Folks spread blankets,
sell onions collards, turnips grown between squeezed sun-ups and
downs. Minah, Ishak, Wolof, Choctaw, Ibo, Creole, Biloxi gather
in self appointed spots. French Quarter bottle-cap tappers mingle
under layers of electric girls just here to twerk.

Musicians ready conga, beat sampler, stool drum, synthesizer,
banjers, and a horse's jaw, teeth played with deer horn.
Rain bullets her scalp, rolls down her neck, settles into collar
hollows. Holy water fonts of her chest, The People dip fingers.

Cross themselves.

She turns, accepts curtsy from Sister Katrina, then skirt in each
fist, snaps upright, arms out. The crowd dies. Silence, length of a
lightning strike, then drums paddle-jump collective heart,
and they begin to move in synch with Oya's machete.

She cuts stillness, spins the wind, and water, newspapers, and
plastic Mardi Gras cups. Tignons fly, releasing curls, and locks,
and inky silk. Gusts lift nine scarves at her waist, one for each
child she's lost. She dances with the storm itself, sorrow holds
hands with hope. Faster, faster, a child's toy on a sidewalk,
bumped back to center by the family ring around her.

Oya

whirls
and she runs,
and she jumps,
her sweat rises,
becomes rain.
She tears it down to the dirt.

Clean for The People. A place to build something better.

Quitting Time at Ruth's Chris Steakhouse

Jimmy Swaggart raises empty glass, rattles his ice.
I arrive, the Buckingham Palace guard of sweet-tea refills.
He hands me check holder, money sticking out the top.
Waiter's station, I unfold the twenty. It's actually a pamphlet.

"Do you love money more than Jesus?"

Louisiana legislator runs laps around dining room
in his boxers. No one looks up. I lean over a polyester shoulder,
to pour water, and a lobbyist bites my tit. Reassigned to run food
I am St. Agatha with my trusty tray.

Boys will be

Out back by the dumpster smoking-lounge I chant-whisper,
Keep your mouth shut, keep your job.
Mouth shut, keep your job.
Keep your mouth shut, keep your job.
Mouthy mouthy, jobby job.

No, I am Phoolan Devi, dusty sari, rifle over shoulder, I toss
order pad full of poems at the feet of Goddess Durga
and start walking.

Magicicada

Time-lapse film shows a cicada
emerge from the dirt
heat darkened classroom smells
of natural gas chalk butter painted lunch rolls

I stare back of the room near supply closet at
beings like me thirteen year
cycles we push from black earth drunk
on Cottonwood sap

Nail bitten fingers skitter under
and over my unhooked bra
tangle in my collar branches
where newborn teens seek safety
a place to shed clunky brown skin

Under jean skirt and translucent
red veined panties that read
Wednesday
two boys shove preying mantid forelegs dip them
in mother's milk of pupal manhood

Later they will raise cupped hands to the faces
of the swarm
prophets spreading good news and the smell
of humiliated flesh

I sit next to my husk under tin roof awning
outside the cafeteria, and make sounds
like electric shocked rattlesnakes
or just a shaken gourd full
of baby teeth

III. The Sweetest Place On Earth

Creole Ladies Don't Do That

Under green awning, corner store,
loose ice melts in a metal bin, sun
throbs on a layer of cubes.
We dig past pineapple, sliced mango, red grapes,
for a plastic bowls of cut watermelon,
fine rectangles nubbily resting in an inch of cold juice.
We walk the sidewalk, shade side, and eat it with
our hands, pink sugar-juice drips down wrists and elbows.
We talk and eat, and walk, mouths open.
We eat and grin big.
In public.
Just like common debris.

Atchafalaya Two-Step

When I die I'll cross the Atchafalaya Bridge
on foot — no cars no aggressive white
F150 on my ass whipping past
cutting me off, cheap plastic
testicles swinging from trailer hitch.

I shuffle step over black rubber snakes,
coiled debris of big rig
blowouts—I10 East, personal path to forever,
through New Orleans, Brest Haiti,
Mama Africa.

Yellow diamond warning says reduce
speed stay in right lane except
to pass. The sun
saffron water balloon filled
with the color of amusement
leaks onto flat water turns scrub pines
into birthday candles.

Do not parle pour parler unless
you prepared to walk
the walk.

mile marker 121.8
The day I ditched a friend, left him sitting
at the bar reading his book, waiting
my shift over — garde manger station
clean, knives in olive army roll, I eased
out the back door.

152
I forgive.

156.8
Someone tried to break in my house
got in cause my screams — were loose.
I sat with my back to the door waiting
honed woman's knife in one hand, cast
iron skillet in the other.

marker 162
I didn't, after all
do my best.

At random mile markers I stop
thread my legs through barrier openings
bare feet slim catfish dangle
over Henderson Swamp

173.2
Stepped on a rusty nail, traiteur called
she said fan myself nine times
with the door of the armoire while standing
in it, and drink a bitter gourd of crushed
roaches steeped in whiskey to unlock
my jaw.

181.5
I forget.

Begin descent.
Bridge splits, a woman
on her back legs spread, her secret
self dressed in cypress.

My apologies, an implorium
of supplications.
I wonder whether they'll be enough
to make the speed limit resume
for me.

Homage to My Hips
(after Lucille Clifton)

What hips?

Boy-slim, I borrow middle school Levis from my son,
can shimmy through drain pipe, retrieve lost dignity, serve you
back to yourself, on a spinning
hubcap.

I step out of shirts without stretching the neck hole,
snake hipped woman, I glide,
belly pressed to earth. Fuck with me, and these hips
will part, legs curve around your chest,
I'll lock ankles, pull a deep breath, squeeze volcanic clouds
from your lungs.

Apartments for Rent on Craigslist

Camped out at a public library table,
they search for an apartment,
for cups of coconut tea, incense stuck in an open windowsill,
luxury of private conversation, no more shouting in faces,
or knees on necks.

"Here's one! Perfect for us.
one bedroom, Uptown, just $1595.00 a month."
Mama sees only sun, her glittered dust motes ride up and down
escalators of light.

Baby Girl endures the moon, fat with responsibility.
Narrowed eyes and crossed arms, help her watch for shady deals,
nocturnal real estate predators.

They shuffle, ready themselves for a grey cloud-walk, bundled,
double hatted, to chase another lead.
Mama heads for the door, empty handed. To her, space
equals freedom.

Baby Girl crams outdated leases, library cards, current resumes,
the sum of their lives into her messenger bag. She carries their
coats, the fierce protector of one whose glass,
is always full.

Lagniappe
for Mikey

Letter penned, algebra class ninth grade.
I don't worry bout my inattention— I was failing anyway.
Baby boy, irrational decision of a girl-child too young to drive
away her demons.
Erzulie's gift, son-shower quenches parched life.

Tore open my gift as children do, believed you "mine"
to pick up or put down, a little something extra.
An offering, eyes solemn, baby-man.

My gift, under the bed missing an arm, wrapped in yellow
bathrobe of genetic sorrow. Creole proverb says "What you lost in
the fire, you'll find in the ashes." So I lay a casket at your feet
filled with matches, and apologies.

What Mama Do

First day of middle school, khaki shorts, navy polo, your lucky bacon socks mid-calf, I kiss your still soft cheek, you slam the screen door. I peek through blinds, egg yolk bus gathers waiting chicks. It turns the corner trailing Hot 97.5 and laughter.

Coffee in hand, I walk the yard, stop to tell secrets to elephant ears. Cypress swing metronomes in the wind. I sit, bare-legged, and lean back.
I Pull up.
Lean back.
Pull up.
Lean back.

Nightgown billows, I launch slippers into freshly cut grass.
And soar.
Legs wide, swing so high I lie back in silent water, head tilted, open mouth gulps a billion molecules. I'll levitate, long as I participate, my own salvation.
Mami Wata holds me suspended, and grounded.

I lie back, starfish on glitter, and swing. Skin boundary disappears.
Upside down,
My coffee cup waits on sidewalk near a grinning crack drinking rain
before breakfast.

The Price of Starting Over

I blow up bridges. Splintered wood and newly
pebbled stone hit water below like summer hail.
Why should I let you in, wrapped in your raggedy
quilt? You swam mud colored rivers to find me.
Time is folded rice paper. You rolled over this
morning, he was gone.
Rumpled sheets mark your legs.
You stand, lost by the creek side.

I'm the gap tooth oracle.
Mother of Chaos, Queen of the Nines.
Shove your wildness into lady pumps.
Amuse me with your middle school wobbles.
Walk to Blind River where slow poured milk
shatters mirrored waters.
Where gnats crash land on eyelids
closed in prayer.

Want your wishes granted? Your questions answered?
Strap your backpack of assumptions to bird boned back.
Blast into magnificent destruction.
The only song for which you know all the words.

Belly

After bathing, we turn sideways, hall mirrors,
catch sight of the sweetest hang-over.
Diastases: the rending of that once joined
divides tightly laced muscle, now canvas pup
tents puckered and twisted by rivulets of dried rain.

Good old shelters, used by feral nomads, to sleep,
dream, tag inner walls with black sharpies, scribble passionate
variations
of self-anointed names.
They wake in the sun, crawl from comfort
womb, lured by distant drums of Mardi Gras Indians.

Spent wigwams list left, Kudzu
covered, swollen with morning-after debris.
Sacred burial mounds in back yards of empty houses.

Yesterday I Was Called A Cunt

Family near the stage during children's production arrived early,
got sous la merde. I asked them to be quiet. Charles Manson's
less attractive twin got up, followed me, leaned
in to my air space, spit one hard syllable between
our faces.

Words penetrate skin, c's and t's slipped into follicles and pores

I am no cunt. No, Padnuh. I am
The Cunt.

Push me against a wall, and I'll drop to my knees,
jump straight up, thighs blasting, and punch you
in the neck.

I'm the cunt who can lead you
by slot machine lever. You'll spill secrets, embedded thorns
of childhood bed wetting, your fear of clowns,
I'll slay you with them later.

I'm the cunt who will read your mail, make your mama love me,
your sister my best friend. Salty bloody midnight cunt,
milky way cunt,
chicken fried cunt,
you'll be my Holofernes, I'll be your Judith.
Hope by now you know, this cunt
will take you down.

Nit Picker

Springtime lice crawl through second grade coat closet,
and my glossy haired friend caught them from her son.
We meet in a park overlooking busy highway, two hot
coffees sit on bench. I bind my hair in hibiscus scarf. Our plastic
hospital gowns flap inna wind.

I micro-part her hair, slide fine tooth metal
comb down silky strands, scalp to tip of precious chicken wings
poking from her sweater.
We talk lovers and dirty diapers, retell stories of us while
I pull fat nits from transparent walnut strands.

I slide them off, snap them between fingernails. We're quiet.
Not like when we weren't speaking. A whole week. I'd cut
her son's hair, thought I did a great job, but she didn't
appreciate my mohawk skills. And how I curled into
poster child for *Abandonment Issues Quarterly* when she failed to
visit after my surgery. She thought herself respectful for not
intruding, demanding.

I comb through acres of thick hair, hear her barking laughter ride
the wind, and know the meaning of "chosen family."

Thunder Wheels

Fweee, fweee
thunder wheels roll through mattress springs.
We pull steam filled blankets over our heads,
let our feet stick out.

Fweee fweee, chick-chock, chick-chock, chick-chock, fweee!
Linen curtains, pregnant with moon breath, let in
tin roof light. It shines through your ear, emblazoned mermaid's toenail,
I fill with words.

Fweee, chhh, fweee
thunder wheels roll, blues, through a party line.
My words drip, they slide down your neck, pool
on your pillow,

swollen words
shiver words
wet-spot words.

Fweee fweee, chick-chock, fweee

thunder wheels roll. I wash you after-words. Slide under your left
arm, my parking spot. 11:10 runs through town; its thunder
wheels rock us
sweat tangled,
into swaddled sleep.

Never Too Old to Fight

On the drive to school, I pat my son's hand, still plump
four dimples above fingers tipped with ragged fish scales.
My hand a trampled atlas of veiny tributaries. I tell myself I have
Georgia O'Keef hands. Hands for heavy turquoise rings fenced
by wide silver cuffs. We Run DMC, at full volume, Subaru
windows vibrate.

Cars wait in horseshoe driveway, my son is slow getting out.
Duty teacher gives him the stink eye, he notices, and drops a
book, she snickers.
I sit up straight, remember how to get rid of hand wrinkles. Make
a fist.
For him I'd give anything I have, and most things I don't.
For him I'd steal a green Cadillac, drive fast enough to launch
over train tracks, scream-laugh till we delete stink-eyes and
snickers.
For him, I'd walk lightless catacombs, find him when he's lost,
give him back to himself, and then drive a hundred miles for
hazelnut gelato.

Our Mother, Who art in Silence

After twelve silent years, Rabb's tree frog begins to sing. His song sandpapers the door of my fortress. I'll bring him home to join the others, last of their kind. They all call for mama in the end. Lonesome George, the Pinta Island Tortise, the Northern White Rhino, the Hawaiian Crow, that sweet Baiji Dolphin, poor blind thing. Whole peoples, animals, trees, rivers. Oh, yes.
Now I remember.

They called me "ruah" in Hebrew, "ruha" in Aramaic, feminine for Holy Spirit.
Me.
Wisdom was MY title.
Once, they knew me. Made in Our image, one for the other, all for all. We, their Father and Mother. Asherah, Ruah, Mother, Mama.

They whispered my name on the hilltops. It hung from Cypress branches like Spanish moss. They screamed for me as they gave birth. Close rooms, windows drawn, the smell of sweat, breath, and amniotic ammonia an effective man repellant. Her last push, my forearm on the bottom of her ribs, her pains rolled through us. I always took half.
Would her Father do that?

Hands hurt in the mornings,
blue veined tributaries run under translucent skin.
Deafening sounds of their loneliness. I hear nothing.
Unloved, separate, unwanted.
Old humans ask their young, "Why don't you ever call?"
They can't help asking.
It is my longing.
I put it there.
It fills vast space inside their atoms, pulses through rivers of blood, a raging wildfire sent to do what wildfires do best...
clear for renewal.

So, children, if you need me, say my name.
Say it when your garden shrivels.
Then look closely for a new spot of green in the dirt.
Sing it to yourself from the dentist's chair.
It's okay Baby, it's just a cavity.
Embroider it on the inside of your leather jacket
so it sits between delicate wing bones.
Imagine my hand there.
Pushing you forward.

Mama. Maman. Ahm. Haha. Madre.

Roar my name in the face of injustice.
Hiss it through locked jaws.
My child meant it when he said he couldn't breathe.
My name, a scalpel, severs loneliness from behind your eyes.
Tattoo it on the bottom of your feet.
I will always hold you upright.
And when you're ready. Really ready for the end,
 like Toughie, let your last breath join the wind.
"Ruah! Asherah, please. Mutti, I need you. Mor, are you there?

Maman? Mama?

Hold on, Sweetie. Shh, doucement. I'm right here.

Sugar in My Bowl:
Post Menopausal Musings (after
Nina Simone)

Saggy and mean, dry, paper brittle, child eater,
whistle blower, hot water thrower, too much information giver.
Papa Legba say, "Child, you want some sugar in your bowl
you know what you gotta do."
You make like Persephone and go down.

Way down.

Under worlds, under skin, your personal hell.
Let night blooming jasmine lead you to grey misted crossroads
where a single bell rings constant Saturn.
Fall on your knees there, open your chest of cedar, toss blood
linens, self lifting skirts, tattered costumes of keep-quiet and
play-along into the mud hole you stomp in the center of the X.

Swim up to the surface, climb out clean and tall. Papa say,
"Now you know, child.
You gotta be the sugar in your own goddamned bowl."

Cartography of a Love Affair

To My Dear Self on Y(our) Wedding Eve,

Look at you. It's past one in the morning and you're still cooking. Stubborn. B tried to talk you out of it. He was more than happy to hire a caterer but you balked at New York City prices, wanted to save the money for the new apartment, asked him what use was a culinary degree if you didn't use it for special occasions. Like I said, stubborn. Mama won't be there tomorrow. Neither will our brother or sister. I'm not telling you anything you don't know. You don't even blame them. You know you don't look like such a catch; on paper. Thirty four years old, divorced, three sons, former teen mother, high school dropout. On our tenth anniversary there'll be a good number of folks who owe each other money. Hey, maybe y'all should have a cardboard Off Track Betting kiosk at the wedding. Not that it would change your minds. Crazy kids.

You've come this far mostly alone but I thought you could use a little support. My wedding gift to you is this map. Follow it, and you'll arrive, eighteen years from now, just in time for beer o' clock. 6 p.m. When B and I sit together for a single beer. We ramble about his constellation lamps, or decide if one of my fictional characters should die violently. Things I still adore about B will serve as mile markers for your journey. Like the sound of drums on Mardi Gras morning, I know you'll recognize them. They'll mark a clear path between you on your bed; one bare foot tucked under your butt and me writing from the hammock in our backyard.

The oldest known map in existence is Babylonian. It shows a round city center with a dot in the middle, which represented a person. The Euphrates River is depicted running through town.

The map, about the size of an iPhone, was not used to navigate from one place to another. Instead, it was a talisman to tuck into a pocket or soft leather bag. It served to remind the bearer that she had a place in the world. She belonged somewhere. So Sister, put on your Easy Spirits and start walking.

His Laugh is Actually a Giggle: The Beginning:
We've established that this isn't your first rodeo.
It is his.
The Guardian of Lost Girls knew only an innocent heart could win yours. Sometimes you look at B and worry you'll only bring him pain. Nine years; lifetimes younger, you hope you're not making one more in a sea of mistakes by deciding to marry him. You aren't.

When you chose him you began the soul process of leveling up. He's doesn't think you need to level up, or down, or side to side. He believes you're already there. B wears spun sugar eyeglasses when it comes to you.
That's good.
Everyone should get to be the sunshine of a life. It took great loss to hone you into the kind of woman who would attract a person like him.

Morning Sun Shines Coral Through His Ears: The Terrain of Trust, practice responding to what's in front of you instead of reacting. You and I are professional reactors. We re-act to experiences familiar to us in the same way we acted in the past. To do this at our skill level one needs to be a champion guesser of intent. It's the way kids learn to protect themselves when adults don't do it for them. And it worked most of the time.

Remember when you were small and could tell how angry your step-father was by the sound of his boots on the linoleum? Or how you stayed bruise free because you divined the courtyard bully's need for praise. That skill doesn't translate well with healthy adults. They don't like being told what they intended. Take B's actions at face value. If you want to know his intent ask him.

Uncross your arms. Let the house get messy. Controlling your world will not keep you safe. It won't guarantee that your friends won't hang you the finger as they slam the door, that you'll never lose a job, or your brother, or your innocence.

Please, beloved, figure out how to connect your mind and body. Pretending you don't have a body is not an option for much longer. I secretly admire the fact that you live on cigarettes, coffee, and donuts, and still have energy to dance all night. For the sake of the baby boy coming your way, maybe you could get a head start on it. Ha! Did I surprise you? Yes indeed, one more son. One more chance to be the kind of mother you thought you couldn't be.

Hang out in libraries and museums. Educate yourself. College is not the only transport to a fulfilling career.

Teach yourself to write. It'll save your life. Then, go out and spark poetry in the bellies of those no one listens to. Watch them vibrate with the power of reading it aloud. The gift of giving new writers your full attention will heal you.

Don't fight sorrow and loss when they show up. Notice I didn't say if, but when. Nobody gets out of here unscathed. Become a conduit so they flow through you, and then move on.

An even harder task: Embrace the joy that you and B will create together. He is worth every side-by-side teeth brushing party. Goofy faces in the mirror. "Hey B! Watch my sexy dance." Know laughter as well as you know hard knocks. Be unable to repeat B's instructions (for the millionth time) about how to use the record player because... the light hit his eyes. And they're moss green. With amber and acorn shards. And those black lashes. Wait. Where was I?

He Mostly Sleeps on His Side of the Bed: Boundaries

All who enter your private thoughts, feelings, orbit, must have a passport. Only you, the ruler of your body can issue a passport. Make sure you're clear about what privileges come with entry. Here in my time, B has more than earned a VIP All-Access lanyard, yet he still must go through customs before being allowed in. The same applies to me. In your time, when B invites you into his inner realms, travel like an emissary on a diplomatic mission. Respecting each other's boundaries will teach your son the value of his own. This is a tender place. Take off your boots before entry.

You've begun to disassemble your ramparts. This is where learning to trust pays off. B's steady presence will inspire you to stay put when you feel like running. He's an envoy clearing space in your heart for others to join him. He's your training wheels for learning to make and keep dear friends.

His Laugh Has Deepened and He Still Holds My Hand: The Middle Ages
Notice I said middle and not end. I know you're tired. Not just from cooking all night. It's okay to rest now. You can rest in B, and he in you, each is the other's platform in the middle of a lake. Go on, nah! Marry your funny, sweet, precious man. You are sincerely loved. By both of us.

Come home, girl.

I'm waiting for you.

Epilogue

A Girl Turns A Doorknob

Dimpled hand hovers over amber doorknob lit from within, a
sign reads: Free Joy Bubbles. No Tricks. Safety Guaranteed.

A girl has no nose for map finding. She slaps her inner compass
on ivory thighs purpled with fingerprints. The arrow swings
in circles, hides coordinates, gives directions New Orleans native
to drunk tourist.

Dimpled hand casts a shadow
of supplication onto door sign. She hesitates.
Could this be the city where upon entry a girl drops her unwashed
fear cloak into an incinerator labeled
Laughter?

A girl spot iridescent fish-scale armor at her feet, near a copy of
worldwide bestseller, Special Air Services Survival Handbook.
Will Vera turn her away? That must be her name; the woman who
commands this place. Though she read the word somewhere,
a girl has no nose for veracity.

Dimpled hand reaches out, then sinks. The beast always finds her,
footsteps pinballing down long hallway. A girl's bravery lies
in her belly bottom. A snarled net of seaweed and hooks and
naked angel fish gulping poison air.

She whispers SOS to the Seven Ferocities:
OYA
Kali
Mami Wata
Ixchel
Anat
Demeter

A girl has no nose for cemented fate. Her prayers waft

through sons & daughters who never found the key to their unlocked cages. Forever captives with phantom keepers. The chant "Stay still. Keep quiet, it'll be over soon."

Dimpled hands shoved in pockets, she starts to walk away, stops, counts realizes she only named six ferocities. So she lifts the armor, tucks the book under her armpit.
Steadies herself. Breathes.

A girl fills her lungs. Vanilla, new socks, her child's sun-warmed hair, goose down comfort, the divot at the base of her man's neck which she calls, "My chin cup."
Now she knows. She drops the armor and stands on it, scales can light through her toes. Aurora Borealis underfoot.

A woman has no nose for anima slaughter.
She is the Seventh Ferocity.
Strong veined, grown ass hand grabs amber doorknob, turns it, and steps inside. She leaves it wide open.

Kelly Clayton is a writer, poet, playwright, and workshop facilitator. She is a Louisiana Creole with roots 15 generations deep. She returned home after twenty years in New York City spent teaching herself to write. Though she dropped out of high school for creative reasons (four sons), she kept both pantry and bookshelves full by working as a waitress, line cook, publisher's assistant, exotic dancer, and event producer. She is a VONA/Voices, Hedgebrook Alumnae, and recipient of the Hedgebrook Women Authoring Change Award. Her poetry has been published by, among others: *Future Cycle Press*, *Delacorte Press*, *China Grove Press*, *The Dead Mule Society of Southern Literature*, and *Random House*. Kelly was awarded an Artist's Residency with the Acadiana Center for the Arts for the production of her original play, "Dancing With Aurora Borealis." Kelly develops and teaches bespoke writing workshops in Louisiana schools, both public and private, for the Lafayette Juvenile Detention Center, and to groups of formerly incarcerated adults. She currently lives in Lafayette with her husband, youngest of four sons, and their Great Pyrenees, Mabelline Wilna Clayton.

Andrew Jolivétte PhD (Creole of Opelousa, Choctaw, Atakapa-Ishak, French, African, Irish, Italian, and Spanish descent), is former professor and chair of the American Indian Studies Department at San Francisco State University. Dr. Jolivétte is the Native American and Indigenous Studies Senior Specialist in the Department of Ethnic Studies at UC San Diego and currently serves as the Board President of the American Indian Community Cultural Center for the Arts in San Francisco, California where he previously served as Executive Director from 2016-2019. He is the author of six books, including *Cultural Representation in Native America* (AltaMira Press, 2006); *Louisiana Creoles: Cultural Recovery and Mixed-Race Native American Identity* (Rowman and Littlefield, 2007); and *Indian Blood: HIV and Colonial Trauma in San Francisco's Two-Spirit Community* (University of Washington Press, 2016), among others. Jolivétte is currently working on a new book manuscript, *Queer Indigenous Citizenship: Against Settler Violence and Anti-Blackness* (University of Washington Press, forthcoming). His first poetry collection, *Gumbo Circuitry: Poetic Routes, Gastronomic Legacies*, will be published by That Painted Horse Press in winter 2021.

Johnathan Wilson's cover art, "Mama Before Coffee" is an original acrylic on canvas. Wilson is a Louisiana born artist currently living in Amsterdam. His illustrations are based on all kinds of fantasy adventure books he loved as a kid. Find him on Instagram: @thefinalbaws